D1506983

OCEAN S.O.S.

J. BURCHETT & S. VOGLER

STONE ARCH BOOKS
a capstone imprint

Wild Rescue books are published by Stone Arch Books
A Capstone Imprint
1710 Roe Crest Drive
North Mankato, Minnesota 56003
www.capstonepub.com

First published by Stripes Publishing Ltd.
1 The Coda Centre
189 Munster Road
London SW6 6AW
© Jan Burchett and Sara Vogler, 2012
Interior art © Diane Le Feyer of Cartoon Saloon, 2012

Cataloging-in-Publication Data is available at the Library of Congress website.

ISBN: 978-1-4342-3771-2 (library binding)

Summary: Ben and Zoe cruise to the Caribbean where a shady marine park
has dumped an unwanted young dolphin into the sea. Having been raised in
captivity, the dolphin is ill-equpped to survive and soon finds itself in troubled
waters. The twins must find the dolphin and guide it to safety before the
confused creature is lost at sea.

Cover Art: Sam Kennedy
Graphic Designer: Russell Griesmer
Production Specialist: Michelle Biedscheid

Design Credits: Shutterstock 51686107 (p. 4-5),
Shutterstock 51614464 (back cover, p. 148-149, 150, 152)

Printed in the United States of America in Stevens Point, Wisconsin.
032013   007240R

TABLE OF CONTENTS

FINGAL

TARGET: ◎

MISSION

BEN WOODWARD
WILD Operative

ZOE WOODWARD
WILD Operative

WILD RESCUE

BRIEFING

CHAPTER 1

DIVING IN

Zoe plunged into the pool just ahead of her twin brother, Ben. They sped through the water until they reached the hot tub, their finishing line. Zoe slapped her hand on the wall.

"I win!" she said.

"Barely," Ben said, panting.

Zoe pushed her brown hair out of her eyes. "What should we do until the wave machine comes on?" she asked.

"More competitions," said Ben. "Bet I can sit on the bottom of the pool and hold my breath longer than you can."

"No thanks," said Zoe. "You always win that one."

But Ben had already sucked in a huge mouthful of air and dived under the surface. Zoe joined him, and they sat on the floor of the pool. Zoe kept her back to her brother, knowing he'd do anything he could to make her laugh.

All of a sudden, someone tapped Ben on the shoulder. He whipped around to see a young woman in dark goggles peering at him. She gave him a thumbs up. Ben let out all his air in a stream of bubbles and burst to the surface with a splash.

Zoe popped up a second later. "I win," she said excitedly.

"I had to come up," Ben said, jerking his thumb over his shoulder. "Erika's here."

Zoe looked up and down the pool. "I can't see her," she said. "You're just making up an excuse for losing to me."

"Over here!" came a voice with a slight German accent. Erika was standing next to a fountain in the corner and waving a glass eyeball at them.

Ben and Zoe swam across to her.

"Hey, Erika!" said Ben. "I take it we've got a new mission?"

Zoe and Ben Woodward were like most other teenagers, except for one important difference: they were operatives for WILD, a secret organization dedicated to saving animals all over the world. It had been set up by their uncle, Dr. Stephen Fisher.

Whenever Zoe and Ben were needed, Uncle Stephen sent his second-in-command, Erika Bohn, to bring them in. But she was never allowed to tell them the details of their mission. Instead, Uncle Stephen always sent them a glass eyeball that served as a clue to which species of animal needed their help.

"Good to see you both," said Erika, smiling brightly. She peeled off her goggles and handed them the glass eyeball. It was about the size of a human's, and had an inky black pupil.

Zoe turned it over in her hand. "I wonder which animal this is from," she muttered.

"You can think about that in the helicopter," said Erika. "Come on, let's get dressed and head to WILD Island."

Twenty minutes later, the three of them were flying out over the ocean. The familiar smell of chicken manure — the helicopter's fuel — filled the air. Like everything at WILD, the chopper was environmentally friendly.

Zoe took the chance to call their grandmother while Ben examined the eyeball. Their parents were vets who were currently working abroad, so their grandma looked after them while their parents were away. Mr. and Mrs. Woodward didn't know that their children worked for WILD. Only Grandma was in on their secret.

"That Stephen," Grandma's cheerful voice said through the speaker. "Where's he sending you now?"

"We don't know yet," said Zoe. "He gave us a clue, though."

"He was always one for a puzzle!" Grandma said with a laugh. "Take care of yourselves, and I'll see you when you get back." The speakerphone cut out.

Ben held up the eyeball. Suddenly, the pupil caught the light and glowed brightly.

"It shines," said Ben. "You know, like a cat or a dog when you shine a light in their eyes. It helps them see in the dark."

Zoe took a look. "What other animals have that?" she asked.

"Quite a few mammals," said Ben. "Including one that lives underwater."

Zoe nodded. "Ben's right," she said. "It could be a dolphin."

Erika pointed toward a hole in the computer's console. "Let's see what your uncle has to say," she said.

Ben placed the eyeball into the slot. At once, a hologram of their uncle appeared.

"Hello, my wonderful nephew and niece," he said. "Have you figured out what it is yet? You might need a clue. It's —"

The image began to flicker. Their uncle's voice flickered in and out. "Something . . . wrong . . . hologram," he sputtered. "Wish I hadn't . . . spilled . . . tea . . . computer." Then the hologram disappeared.

Zoe laughed. "Uncle Stephen may be brilliant, but he's pretty clumsy," she said. "I guess we'll just have to wait."

"WILD Island coming up," Erika said as she brought the helicopter down for a landing.

As soon as they'd exited the chopper, Erika pressed a button on a handheld remote, activating a mechanism.

Suddenly, a fake shed rose around them to hide the helicopter. Then they made their way to an outhouse, that was, in fact, a secret elevator.

Ben and Zoe felt their stomachs lurch as they zoomed down into the headquarters of WILD. When the elevator doors opened, they found themselves face to face with their uncle. He was wearing a lab coat over bright shorts, with a funny hat atop his messy hair.

"Greetings, children!" Uncle Stephen cried. "Now come with me, there's no time to lose."

They hurried down the hallway. Next to a door marked CONTROL ROOM, they all took turns placing their fingertips on a small pad. As soon as their prints had been identified, the door slid open.

Now they stood in front of a large, bright room that was the headquarters of WILD. Consoles and lights flashed. Operatives clicked away at keyboards, but they all paused to smile and wave at Ben and Zoe. The two of them had developed quite a reputation among the WILD employees after all their daring rescues.

Uncle Stephen led Ben and Zoe over to his desk. "Sorry about the hologram," he said. "Were you able to figure out what animal the eye belongs to?"

"Well, we're pretty sure it's a mammal," Ben said.

"And?" Uncle Stephen asked.

"That's not much to go on," Erika said. "Maybe you should give them another clue."

Uncle Stephen stroked his chin. "Although this animal is a mammal," he said, "it lives in the sea, and it's particularly intelligent."

Ben opened his mouth to speak, but before he could, Zoe cried out. "I knew it," she said. "We're rescuing a dolphin!"

"Nice work," said Uncle Stephen. "I knew you two would discover the answer!"

CHAPTER 2

DOLPHIN DILEMMA

Zoe tugged at their uncle's sleeve. "Tell us the details!" she said impatiently.

"I want you to look at this," said Uncle Stephen. He pointed to a huge wall monitor displaying a website for a marine park. The park looked bright and welcoming, with the slogan "Mundo Marino, the jewel of the Caribbean Coast" on top of the webpage.

"We have an operative who keeps track of what goes on in water parks and zoos all over the world," Uncle Stephen explained.

"Recently, she picked up reports of problems at this place in Mexico," added Erika. "It used to be run by an old man who loved all forms of marine life."

Uncle Stephen continued the story. "He died six months ago, so his son took it over," he said. "He didn't spend enough money on the park and if any member of staff complained, he fired them. By the time the authorities found out and closed it down, many animals were in terribly unhealthy."

"That's horrible!" said Ben.

"It gets worse," Uncle Stephen said. "Of the four bottlenose dolphins there, only one four-year-old male named Fingal was still alive. And he has a scar running from his right eye to just below his mouth, so he must have been mistreated."

"That's awful," said Zoe. "So we need to rescue Fingal. But if the park was closed down, where is he now?"

"We don't know," said Erika. "When the owner found out the authorities were after him, he dumped all the animals in the ocean. Most of the animals were born in captivity and won't be able to survive in the wild."

"So he could be anywhere in the Caribbean by now," said Ben.

"We don't think he's gone far," said Uncle Stephen, "and that's part of the problem."

Uncle Stephen tapped a key, bringing a map of the Caribbean Sea to the screen. He indicated a point on the southeast coast of Mexico. "San Miguel," he said. "That's where Fingal was dumped four days ago."

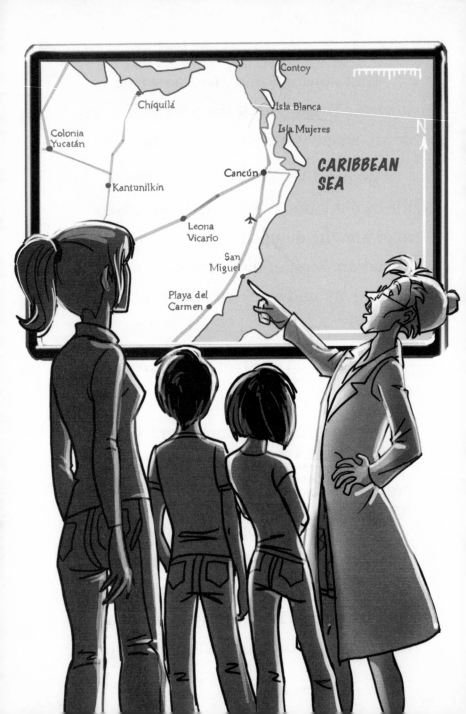

"We've been monitoring local radio reports," Uncle Stephen said, "and it seems that a young dolphin has been harassing fishermen in San Miguel. We think this must be Fingal. He seems to be after their fish."

"Fingal was born in the park, so he would naturally go to humans for his food," said Erika.

"The fishermen won't like that," said Zoe.

"You're right," said Uncle Stephen. "And that's why your mission is so urgent. Fingal will either get hurt or caught in a net if he's not rescued soon. And there's always the danger of a shark attacking a young dolphin that isn't protected by a pod."

Erika nodded and added, "Fingal needs rehabilitation before it'll be safe for him to live in the wild," she said.

"Who does that kind of rehabilitation?" asked Ben.

"The Agua Clara Dolphin Sanctuary is about 100 miles from there," said Uncle Stephen, "but they don't have the time or resources to travel that far to search for a dolphin in trouble."

A sly grin crawled across their uncle's face. "However, I can think of one way they would find him very quickly," he said. "If he were tracked down and encouraged to sit still for a while, then maybe the center could come and get him."

"Well, Ben," Zoe said, winking at her twin brother. "I wonder who our uncle has in mind for this challenging task?"

"I suppose we could do it, Zoe," Ben said with a grin. "We're not very busy lately, and it is summer vacation."

Uncle Stephen smiled at them. "I knew my wonderful nephew and niece would be up for it."

"When do we leave for San Miguel?" asked Zoe eagerly.

"We'll be leaving as soon as you've got all of your equipment," said Erika. "I'll pretend to be your aunt who is taking you along on vacation while I work. I'm going to pose as an environmentalist."

"You *are* an environmentalist!" Uncle Stephen said with a laugh. He turned to Ben and Zoe. "Her reason for being in a Mexican fishing village is real. I've been looking into the problem of dolphins being caught in fishing nets for some time. There are devices that mimic the call of a much larger marine mammal so that dolphins are warned to stay well away."

"But those devices can be too expensive for poor fishing communities like those around the San Miguel area," Erika added.

"That's right," Uncle Stephen said with a nod. "So I've developed my own version that is much cheaper and just as effective."

"I'm going to offer the fishermen a free trial," said Erika. "And while I'm doing that, you can search for Fingal."

"Will we get to do some snorkeling?" Ben asked.

Uncle Stephen rubbed his hands together. "You certainly will," he said. "And you'll be using my latest invention to do it."

He opened a drawer and rummaged through it for a few moments. Finally, he pulled out two snorkels and some flippers, and then handed them to Ben and Zoe.

"Snorkels have already been invented, Uncle Stephen," Zoe said, smiling.

"These may look like normal snorkels," said their uncle, "but they're not. They're GILS — Great Integrated Life Support. Unlike a snorkel, this will give you ten minutes of oxygen." Uncle Stephen pointed to Zoe's device. "See the little capsule there in the mouthpiece? This is a special compressed air tank. All you have to do is go back up to the surface and it refills automatically. I've set it to give you a strong taste of peppermint when the air is about to run out so you have a warning. And if you look closely at the mask, you'll see it's designed to give improved underwater visibility."

"And let me guess," said Ben, pointing at the flippers. "These are no ordinary flippers, either."

"Indeed," Uncle Stephen said, smiling. "They're extra streamlined for increased speed."

"Cool!" said Ben. He slipped on the flippers and waddled round the room. "They feel really light — and strong."

"What sort of boat will we be using?" asked Zoe.

"A speedboat?" said Ben hopefully.

"Don't be silly, Ben," Zoe said with a laugh. "The engine would frighten Fingal away."

"Zoe's right," said Erika. "I'll be renting a sailing dinghy for you."

"Perfect!" Zoe said, pumping her fist in the air.

Ben grinned. "You would say that," he said.

"I bet right now you're wishing you'd taken those sailing courses with me last summer," said Zoe.

Erika opened Uncle Stephen's drawer. After removing two apple cores and an old milk carton, she produced what looked like two handheld game consoles and held them out to Ben and Zoe. "Of course you can't go without your BUGs," she said.

Ben and Zoe's BUGs were impressive little gadgets. They had built-in radios and phones, satellite trackers, translators, and countless other useful gadgets. They even had one or two video games, which Ben loved.

"Wait a minute," said Ben. "Are these still going to work in the ocean?"

"They're waterproof," said Uncle Stephen. "I've tested them in my bathtub!"

Ben and Zoe groaned.

"I've also added a limpet," Uncle Stephen said, ignoring them. "It's a wireless extension of your BUGs."

Zoe turned her BUG over in her hand. She peeled off a coin-sized piece of rubber with a metal device embedded in it. "Is this it?" she asked.

"Yep," said Uncle Stephen. "It's designed to stick to the side of your boat by giving off a slimy substance, just like a real limpet does. It transmits and identifies calls underwater. All the info will be displayed on your BUG screens."

"Awesome," said Zoe.

"You'll also have a supply of treats to lure Fingal to you," Erika added.

"I made up the recipe," Uncle Stephen said. "They're only tasty to dolphins."

"Good," said Zoe. "Otherwise Ben would eat them all!"

Ben smiled. "She's probably right," he said with a shrug.

"Time for you to leave," said Uncle Stephen. "The WILD jet is fueled and ready to go — and Fingal is depending on you."

"I think there's something you forgot to tell them, Dr. Fisher," said Erika.

"What's that?" Uncle Stephen asked.

"The weather?" Erika said as she raised her left eyebrow.

"Oh yes!" said their uncle. He turned to face Ben and Zoe. "One other thing — it's hurricane season in the Caribbean." Uncle Stephen frowned. "I hope that won't scare you off," he said.

"No way!" said Zoe. "Fingal, here we come!"

CHAPTER 3

SAN MIGUEL

Zoe looked out the guest house window at the clear blue sky. She pulled on her shirt and shorts over her wetsuit. "It's a lovely day," she said. "Light breeze, good sailing weather — perfect for our mission."

They had arrived with Erika at the Casa Blanca guest house in San Miguel late the night before. The hotel's owner, Señor Rodriguez, had greeted them and given them hot drinks and a big plate of cookies.

"Come on, Zoe," said Ben impatiently. "Let's get going."

"Don't be so hasty," Zoe said. She sat on her bed and lifted her backpack up beside her. "We've gotta do a final check of our equipment first." She rummaged through her bag. "First-aid kit, binoculars, GILs . . ."

". . . flippers, diving belt with knife, treats for Fingal," muttered Ben, carefully repacking each one. "How's your Spanish?"

"I can say please and thank you," said Zoe.

"Can you say, 'do you know where the missing dolphin is because we've come to rescue him and get him to a rehabilitation center?'" Ben said with a smirk.

Zoe rolled her eyes. "I'll leave that to you!" she said.

Ben picked up his BUG and peeled off a small plastic earpiece from the side. "At least with our translators we can make sure that we understand everything we hear," he said, stuffing it in his ear.

Zoe did the same and they turned on their BUGs' translation mode.

Just then, Ben's BUG vibrated. "Message from Erika," he said. "Sailing dinghy rented. It's down on the pier."

"I wonder how her meeting with the fishermen is going," said Zoe, tucking her flippers, mask, and snorkel into her bag. "Good thing she's fluent in Spanish, since she has to explain how Uncle Stephen's complicated nets work!"

Erika had wasted no time. Immediately after breakfast, she had departed for a large fishing village along the coast.

Erika planned to start her campaign of persuading the fishermen to use the new nets right away, so Ben and Zoe were on their own already.

Ben hoisted his backpack on to his shoulders. "Let's see what we can find out about Fingal from the local people," he said.

"Good idea," said Zoe, as they made their way down to the lobby. "Make sure to be subtle about it. They can't know we're from WILD."

Ben rolled his eyes. "Duh," he said. "Anyway, while we're in the village we should buy some food."

"You just had breakfast!" said Zoe. "You can't still be hungry. The hot chocolate and spicy tortillas were delicious — and very filling."

"Yep," Ben said. "And that's why I'm already looking forward to lunch!"

Señor Rodriguez came out. He glanced at the children's bulging backpacks. "Are you going on a long trip?"

"We're going sailing," said Zoe. "Our aunt's renting us a boat. The sea looks very clear here — not like back home — and we want to see the underwater life."

"My sister has always dreamed of seeing wild dolphins," Ben added, taking up the cover story. "If we don't see any, I'll never hear the end of it!"

"You're in luck," said Señor Rodriguez. "The fishermen often see dolphins from their boats. But listen, your aunt might not have to take you that far out. You might even see the dolphin from the old marine park."

"What do you mean?" asked Zoe, pretending to be clueless. Ben admired how good she'd become at acting since they started working for WILD.

Señor Rodriguez told them all about the closing of the marine park.

"The dolphin's been popping up ever since," Señor Rodriguez said. "Only yesterday, Filiberto told me it had been pestering him when he was fishing. It was a real nuisance. It kept calling to him and banging against the side of the boat. Then it did a funny sort of backward walk on its tail."

"That does sound like a tame dolphin," said Zoe, giving Ben a knowning glance.

"You be careful now," Señor Rodriguez added. "Dolphins are pretty friendly, but there are also sharks further out in the bay. So no swimming out there, okay?"

"We'll look out for sharks," Ben said, nodding.

Ben and Zoe headed toward the sea. They walked along a rough, dusty road toward the center of San Miguel.

In this area, houses were scattered around an old church. The morning sun warmed the red-tiled roofs.

Ben and Zoe turned a corner and gasped in delight. Ahead of them lay the turquoise waters of the Caribbean, sparkling in the sunshine. A few guest houses and tourist shops overlooked the ocean, but there were no tourists around. The bay was wide, with a wooden pier. Nearby, boats tethered to red buoys bobbed in the gentle swell. Several fishing vessels were heading toward shore to haul in their catches of the day. Ben and Zoe could hear the distant drone of their engines as they puttered in. Far out to sea, the twins could barely make out a small island that was scattered with palm trees.

"That's a coral island," Ben said. "I read about them on the plane."

Zoe aimed her binoculars at the far end of the bay, where a battered fence surrounded some shabby buildings. A tattered sign hung loosely on its hinges.

"That's Mundo Marino," Zoe said in disgust. "So that's where poor Fingal was living."

"Soon we'll get him to a much better place than that," said Ben.

They made their way down the main street. They passed gift shops, a bar, and several grocery stores. Nearly all of the shop owners were placing wooden shutters over the windows. "Everyone's closing their stores," Zoe said, surprised.

One small store still had the door open. "At least we can buy our food here," said Ben. He pushed open the door and breathed in the delicious smell of freshly baked bread and smoked meats.

"Hello," Zoe said to the woman behind the counter. "Do you speak English?"

"A little," the woman said.

"Why is everything closing?" Zoe asked, pointing to the shutters.

"Hurricane," the woman said with an apologetic smile.

Zoe turned to Ben. "This is really bad news," she whispered in alarm. "Fingal isn't used to being in the ocean, let alone in hurricane conditions."

"We've got to get Fingal to the center before the hurricane arrives," Ben whispered. "If he stays near the shoreline, he'll find it hard to swim in the strong waves. He could get hurt, or killed."

"Let's hope there's enough time," whispered Zoe.

CHAPTER 4

HURRICANE

"We need to find out when the hurricane is going to hit," Ben said. "Hurry up and pick what you want. Then we'll ask."

Zoe quickly grabbed fruit, crackers, and bottles of water. Ben pointed to the biggest pastry on display. It was stuffed with chicken and cream cheese.

"Pastelitos," said the shop owner, as she wrapped two up. "Very good."

"When is the hurricane coming?" Zoe asked as she paid.

"Hurricane is come . . . is . . ." The woman gave up her attempt at English and led them to the door. She nodded toward a nearby café. There was a terrace outside, where a man was working. All the tables and chairs had been cleared away.

"Good English!" she said, pointing at the café owner as he hung the last shutter. "He tell you."

They thanked her and dashed for the café. The trees were swaying a little in the breeze, and the sky was blue, but hurricanes weren't exactly known for coming on slowly.

The café owner smiled as they approached. He was a friendly looking man with brown eyes above a well-groomed moustache.

"Can you help us?" asked Zoe. "We've heard there's a hurricane coming, but the weather looks so calm."

"We might be at the edge of one," the man told them. "So we take precautions. The National Hurricane Center's report said it will pass close by this afternoon, but we need to make sure we are ready just in case."

"That's a relief," said Zoe. "We should be able to get some sailing in this morning, then."

"You don't seem too worried about the storm," said Ben to the café owner.

The man gave a shrug. "We are used to it," he said. "The storm comes, we close up shop. The storm goes, we open up again. What else can we do?"

At that moment, a man in fisherman's overalls stuck his head out the door and called out to the owner in Spanish.

Ben and Zoe's BUGs translated the words. "News just in, Enrico. The hurricane's heading north. It's going to miss us this time."

Enrico told Ben and Zoe the news. "You will be able to enjoy your sailing," he said. He began to take down the shutters from the window. "And if you see some strange dead fish, do not worry. There is nothing wrong with the water. They were, how do you say . . . thrown out from Mundo Marino."

"We've heard about that," said Ben, a grim look on his face.

"But be careful of the tame dolphin," Enrico warned them. "It could tip over a small boat. The fishermen are angry at it."

"They won't hurt the dolphin, will they?" said Zoe.

The café owner shrugged. "Making a living is hard enough here," he said. "I wouldn't be surprised if it ended up getting killed."

Zoe couldn't hide the fear in her face. "Don't worry," Enrico said. "I'm sure the little fella will find some friends and leave the area soon enough."

"Gracias," Zoe said to the café owner. "Thanks for your help."

The owner smiled, turned, and walked away.

"Poor Fingal," Zoe said to Ben once the man had left. "All he's trying to do is survive."

"And that's all the fishermen are trying to do," Ben said. "We have to do something, and soon."

CHAPTER 5

LA GAVIOTA

Ben and Zoe raced along the rough bay road toward the wooden pier stretching out from the beach.

"I really wish I'd taken those sailing classes with you," Ben said, panting as they ran. "But baseball seemed like more fun at the time."

"Don't worry," Zoe said. "Just do what I tell you, and we'll be fine."

"Great!" said Ben. "Another excuse to boss me around."

There was a worn sign in English and Spanish that read "boats for rent" with an arrow pointing down the pier.

A small, single-masted sailing boat was tethered at the end. Its green paint was peeling, and two narrow benches ran along the inside. A dark-haired woman waved at Ben and Zoe as they neared the pier.

"That's our boat," said Zoe. "*La Gaviota.*"

"Looks pretty basic," said Ben, "but it's just the right size for the two of us."

"Boat for Erika Bohn?" the woman said in English. "Rented for one day's hire?"

"That's right," said Zoe eagerly.

"Your aunt said you can sail," the woman said. She looked at them doubtfully. "But you're so young."

Ben gulped nervously.

Zoe nudged Ben in the ribs. "I have taken sailing classes," Zoe said truthfully.

"That is good," the woman said. She handed them two life jackets. "You must wear these always. That is the rule."

Ben and Zoe slipped on the orange jackets.

Zoe bent down, pulled in the rope attached to the boat, and held the pointed front of the boat firmly. She dropped their two backpacks into the bottom of the boat and nodded to her brother. "Go ahead, Ben," she said. "Climb aboard."

The boat owner folded her arms and watched. It was clear that she was worried about her craft being safe in the hands of two children.

It didn't help that Ben stumbled as he climbed onto the dinghy, making it rock violently.

"Whoa!" Ben said, his arms flailing. He grabbed the mast and clung to it desperately.

"My brother likes to joke," Zoe said quickly. Ben threw himself onto one of the benches and gave a sheepish grin.

Zoe noticed that the woman didn't return the smile. But before she could say anything, Zoe swiftly untied the rope and boarded the boat. First she rigged the sails. Then she climbed to the stern and took hold of the tiller. As the sails caught the wind, she headed the boat out into the middle of the bay.

"Close one," said Ben, looking back. "But she's still staring at us. What can I do to show her how much of an expert I am?"

"Take that sheet and control the jib," Zoe told him, nodding toward the small triangular sail at the prow.

Ben reached forward and grabbed the bottom of the front sail.

Ben wrestled with the flapping canvas. "I'm not sure I can hold on for long," he said. "It's pulling away."

Zoe burst out laughing. "The sheet is the rope that controls a sail," she said. "It's down there, secured to the side. Release it from its cleat — or clip, to landlubbers like you."

"Very funny!" Ben said. He freed the rope and grinned at her. "I'd like to see you explain the sacrifice fly rule from baseball!"

"Anyway, it's time for business," Zoe said. "We have to search this bay for Fingal. We'll start looking around those fishing boats over there. Get ready to let go of your rope when I tell you, then move to the other side of the dinghy."

Ben ducked around the boom.

"Oh, and watch your head," Zoe warned. "The big wooden beam will swing across."

"The boom, you mean?" said Ben. "I do know that one!" His feet kicked something under the seat and he pulled it out. It was a pail attached to a long piece of rope, which was tied to a hook. "A bucket?" he asked. "Is that in case we're seasick?"

"It's for bailing out water, silly," said Zoe. "Hang our backpacks on that hook, too. Everything has to be battened down." She looked ahead. "Okay, ready about?"

"Show off," said Ben.

Zoe grinned. "Look out, we're turning," she said. She pushed the tiller away from her.

The boom moved over the boat. Ben raised the sheets on the other side. Taken by the gentle wind, the dinghy moved among the rocking fishing boats that were attached to buoys in the water.

Ben slipped his BUG out of his backpack, scrolled through the animal identification menu, and set it to pick up dolphin calls. Then he peeled the limpet from his BUG and reached over the side of the boat.

Ben attached the limpet to the hull just beneath the waterline. "Nothing yet," Ben said, peering at the BUG screen.

"Let's get farther out and try again," said Zoe. She adjusted the mainsail to catch the light breeze.

As they reached the last buoy before they would reach open sea, a message appeared on Ben's screen. "The limpet's picked something up," he said. "It's a dolphin — and it's close!"

They peered eagerly over the water. Just a few yards away, the surface erupted as a sleek gray dolphin leaped up in an elegant arc. Then it plunged back into the waves. They could see it streaking through the clear water close to the boat.

Zoe's eyes went wide. "Could that be Fingal?" she said.

"It looks like an adult," said Ben doubtfully.

As he spoke, more fully grown dolphins burst to the surface. "It's a pod!" said Zoe. "Of course, now that we're a ways out, we're going to see lots of dolphins!"

The streamlined shapes shot along next to the dinghy, launching themselves out of the water and diving back with barely a splash.

"It's like they're racing us!" said Ben.

"Not much of a race," Zoe said. "They're a lot faster than this boat is. They're just tagging along for the ride."

The dolphins criss-crossed in the air in front of the boat. Then, as suddenly as they had come, they were gone.

"How amazing," she said softly. "They were so beautiful!"

Ben grinned. "Cuteness overload," he said with a groan. "Although I have to agree that they were amazing."

"Wouldn't it be great if Fingal was a part of a group like that?" asked Zoe.

Ben nodded. "That's the goal," he said. "But we'd better wait a while before we try to listen for him again. We'll just end up locating that pod again."

"I'll head toward the bay," said Zoe. "He must be there somewhere."

CAUGHT

Ben and Zoe sailed up and down between the buoys, but no alerts appeared on the BUG screen.

"I think we're in the wrong place," said Ben. "We've been searching for over an hour and there's still no sign of Fingal."

Suddenly, they heard a distant shout from across the water. They looked up to see a small boat out beyond the bay. They could hear the chug of its engine.

"A fishing boat," said Zoe. "It must be coming back with its catch."

Then there was silence as someone turned the power off. "Looks like they've got a problem with their net," said Ben.

Two of the crew were desperately trying to pull up a bright green fishing net. A third person called out instructions while keeping the lurching vessel balanced.

Ben and Zoe could make out a few words, translated by the BUG.

"Something's caught," one voice said.

"It's big," said another.

"It's struggling!" a third voice warned. "It'll tip us over."

Ben got out his binoculars and looked through them. "Can't see what they've picked up," he reported anxiously, "but it's certainly in trouble."

Zoe glanced down at Ben's BUG screen.

"We should have checked sooner," Zoe
said. "It's saying 'dolphin'!"

"It could be Fingal," said Ben. Zoe
swung the boat around and edged it
toward the struggling fishermen.

"The BUG identified it as a distress cry,"
Ben said. "Even if it's not Fingal, we've got
to get in there and do something."

Ben pressed some buttons on his BUG. "I'm saving that dolphin's call just in case," he said. "All dolphins have a different signature call, and if this is Fingal, we'll be able to identify him from now on."

Zoe steered the dinghy toward the buoys in the bay. Lowering the sails, she secured the boat to the nearest one while Ben got out their GILS and flippers.

"If only I had my sailing knife with me," said Zoe. "We could use it to cut the net."

"I've got something even better," said Ben. "My diver's knife." He produced a sheathed knife from the backpack and strapped it to his belt.

"Remember what Señor Rodriguez told us," said Zoe. "Keep an eye out for sharks."

Ben nodded. He ripped off his life jacket and clothes. "I don't need to be told twice," he muttered. Ben pulled the mask on and adjusted the snorkel. Then he attached his BUG to his diving belt with a safety cord. Zoe did the same.

"Don't forget, you only have ten minutes of air," Zoe said.

Ben made a circle with his thumb and forefinger — the diver's sign for OK — and plunged into the water with a splash.

The water rushed into his ears as he sank into the clear sea. Bubbles streamed up in front of his face. When the bubbles cleared, he spotted the long, dark shape of the fishing boat in the water ahead. With the GILS, he was able to breathe just as if he had an oxygen tank.

The water was very clear, so Ben made sure that he kept on the side of the boat away from the fishermen so they wouldn't see him. But now he had a good view of the net. It was full of fish, and thrashing violently. As he came closer he could just see the terrified eye of a dolphin in the middle of the catch.

Zoe was approaching. Ben jerked a thumb up, and they swam for the surface, making sure to stay out of sight of the fishermen.

"The dolphin is badly tangled in the fishing net," Ben told his sister as he treaded water next to her. "The more it tries to free itself, the worse it gets. There's no way it can escape on its own."

"Poor thing," said Zoe. "Is it Fingal?"

"Can't tell," said Ben. "We'll have to go back down to check. I'll use my knife to cut it free, but we can't let the fishermen see us."

"Agreed," said Zoe. "We'll approach from underneath the hull — but stay far away from its propeller."

Together, they dived under the bottom of the fishing boat.

Zoe checked for holes in the nylon mesh. After a few moments, she shook her head at Ben.

Ben held the net to steady himself as he pulled his knife from its sheath. The net gave a big lurch, and the dolphin's head appeared as it pushed its nose desperately against its prison.

Ben tugged at Zoe's arm. He pointed to a jagged scar running from the dolphin's eye to just below its mouth.

They had found Fingal!

CHAPTER 7

BLOOD IN THE WATER

This isn't working, thought Ben as he worked at the net with his knife. *The more frightened Fingal becomes, the more he tangles himself up. If we don't free him soon, he'll run out of air.*

Cutting a net underwater would have been slippery work even without a terrified dolphin around. Each time Ben tried to break the net, Fingal would thrash. Ben had lost his grip on his knife several times. *Good thing it's attached to my belt,* he thought.

Fingal writhed again and Ben nicked his hand with the knife. A slim stream of blood trailed through the water from the cut. Ignoring the stinging pain, he attacked the net again and managed to slice through two strands.

Fingal's struggles were slowing down the rescue attempt. Zoe swam to where his head was caught.

He stared at her for a moment with frantic eyes, then started wriggling again. Zoe touched his snout through the net and patted his head.

Fingal calmed down a little. Ben cut through another strand, then another. Then he tugged at the broken threads.

Zoe helped Ben tear at the thick nylon net. Suddenly, Fingal poked his snout through the hole. Ben and Zoe ripped the hole wider. They could feel the harsh nylon digging into their hands.

At last, they managed to drag it over the dolphin's head. After another tug, his flippers were free. But now the net was caught on his dorsal fin. Ben and Zoe grabbed the net and pulled hard. With a flick of his tail, Fingal burst through the hole and toward the surface.

But now, Ben was worried. When the fishermen saw the young dolphin and the hole in their net, they might be angry enough to do something nasty to him.

The net was rising slowly through the water, fish spilling out as the men winched it up. Zoe swam up on the other side of the boat to look for Fingal and lure him away. There he was, leaping in and out of the water, trying to attract the attention of the fishermen. Luckily, they were too busy cursing at the loss of their catch to notice him.

Zoe waved frantically at Fingal and then dived under the water. Thankfully, the dolphin came swimming toward her.

Fingal gave Zoe what looked like a smile, nudged her gently in the tummy, and then swam on his back.

Zoe dived down deeper, and Fingal followed.

Then Zoe saw Ben. He was fiddling with the net still. The cord securing his knife to his belt had gotten tangled in it. He was stuck!

Ben struggled desperately to free his knife. If he unclipped the cord and swim away, he'd leave the knife in the nylon mesh. If he did that, then the fishermen would be sure to see the knife when they pulled the net up, meaning they'd know that the net had been tampered with.

Ben couldn't risk losing his knife, either. It was likely that he and Zoe would need it again before this adventure was over.

Then Ben tasted peppermint. The GIL was running out of air — they'd have to surface soon. Ben signaled to Zoe that his oxygen was running out. He desperately began to tear at the net, holding his breath. Ben was good at that, but how long could he last?

Ben turned when Zoe's hand touched his.

Zoe worked with nimble fingers, nudging Fingal away when he got too close. At last, she got the knife free. And just in time — the net shot up above the surface, sending Ben somersaulting backward through the water.

Ben and Zoe were just about to kick away from the boat when a tremendous roar filled their ears and the water churned around them. The propeller was beginning to turn. Now that what was left of the catch was in their boat, the fishermen had started the engine.

Whoosh! Fingal was gone, terrified by the noise and sudden swirling in the water. Above them, the boat began to move. Ben kicked away hard to avoid the blades. He thrashed to the surface and gulped the air in relief.

Zoe swam up alongside him. "Are you all right?" she asked.

"I'm fine," said Ben, "now that I'm finally breathing some fresh air."

"Where's the blood coming from?" Zoe asked.

Ben looked at the cut on his hand. "It's nothing," he said. "I just nicked myself with my knife. The important thing is that we find Fingal."

"We'll be able to search for him better when we're back in the dinghy," said Zoe. "He can't be very far away."

As they swam, Ben looked around. "You're right, I think I can see his fin," he said, pointing at the horizon. "And he's heading toward us at pretty fast."

Zoe treaded water and checked her BUG. "That's not Fingal," she said, her eyes going wide. "In fact it's not a dolphin at all. Swim for the boat!"

"What's the matter?" asked Ben.

"It's a shark!" Zoe yelled out.

CHAPTER 8

SHARK!

Ben and Zoe thrashed through the waves, the water pounding in their ears. Even with their super-fast flippers, they were no match for the expert underwater killer that was rocketing toward them, attracted by the blood leaking from Ben's finger.

Ben couldn't stop himself from taking a quick glance backward under the surface. He wished he hadn't when he caught sight of the shark's tiny eyes and needle-sharp teeth.

Ben was sure it would reach them before they could get to safety. He kicked desperately, swimming for his life.

Zoe reached the dinghy first. Ben saw her legs disappearing from the water as she scrambled aboard. With a final burst of energy, he launched himself at the boat. He felt a surge behind him as the shark lunged for him.

Ben grabbed the edge of the dinghy and tried to pull himself up out of the water. In his panic he lost his grip on the side of the boat and plunged back into the water. He could see the ominous gray shape of the shark circling beneath him, returning to attack. The blood from his hand was trailing out in a thin ribbon, exciting the hungry predator. Ben clawed at the side of the dinghy and kicked in desperation.

Then, just as the shark lunged, Zoe clutched his arm and pulled him to safety.

Ben tumbled onto the deck just as the shark smashed into the boat's hull. He lay there, panting, while Zoe clung fearfully to the side and watched the gray body whipping around below them, battering the craft in frustration.

"We've got to get away!" Ben said. "It could capsize the dinghy."

Shaking, Zoe climbed onto her seat, pulled off her snorkelling gear, and raised the sails. Soon, the dinghy was coasting over the waves, away from the bay. But the shark wasn't giving up. Its gray fin could be seen copying every course change they made.

Ben scrolled down the menu of his BUG. "It's a bull shark," he read from the screen. "They often attack without having a reason. So my blood must have really stirred it up."

"It's coming straight for us," yelled Zoe.

"It's going to ram us again!" cried Ben.

The shark slowed just before it reached them and swerved away. "That must have been a practice run," said Zoe. "Look, it's coming again."

"I'll find a predator call to scare it," said Ben. He scrolled through the BUG menu, his fingers typing keys quickly.

Now the shark was almost upon them.

"I set the limpet to give out a killer whale sound," Ben said quickly. "I hope it works, since the bull shark isn't frightened by many creatures."

The sound must have reached the shark, because it suddenly changed course. With a flick of its powerful tail, it disappeared from view.

Zoe sighed. "Good thinking," she said.

"Thanks for earlier," Ben said. "You saved my life."

Zoe shrugged. "Who's going to scrub the decks if my cabin boy gets eaten?" she said.

Ben laughed. "I'll do it the minute we've found Fingal," he said.

"That's not going to be so easy," said Zoe seriously. "He was really scared by that boat engine. He could be far away by now."

"Remember what the lady at the rental place told us," Ben said as he threw Zoe her life jacket.

They both put them back on, tying the straps firmly. Suddenly, they heard an engine. "Look out," said Ben. "There's a cabin cruiser coming."

"Ahoy there!" came a cry.

A man stood at the cruiser's prow. The vessel came alongside and they heard the engine slowing.

"Don't forget, we're just dumb tourists," Zoe muttered to Ben.

The man peered down at *La Gaviota* over the side of his cruiser. A woman wearing dark sunglasses stood next to him.

"Do you speak English?" the man called loudly. He had an English accent.

Zoe grinned. "Sure do," she said.

"We thought we would check on you," said the man.

"We were surprised to see you out here," added the woman. "You're very young to be out on your own."

"Don't worry about us," called Ben in a pleasant voice. "My sister's an expert sailor. She has all sorts of badges."

"We're just having a little sailing practice," said Zoe.

"I'm teaching my brother the basics, so we're staying out of the bay to avoid the other boats," Zoe chimed in, picking up the cover story. "He's taking a long time to learn."

The woman laughed as Ben pretended to get himself tangled up in the ropes.

"Well, don't go out any farther," said the man. "Stefano, our captain, told us that there's a hurricane on its way. It's not going to hit the coast, but it'll pass quite close and you'll feel the effects if you head into deeper water. You'd better follow us back to San Miguel. We're heading in now, just to be on the safe side."

Zoe and Ben were silent for a moment, trying to think of what to say. "That's really kind of you," said Zoe at last. "But we . . . but . . ."

"But our aunt's not far away in her boat," Ben said quickly. "We'll wait and sail in with her. But thanks anyway."

"Your aunt?" said the woman doubtfully. "We didn't see any other small dinghies."

"Are you sure?" said Ben. He slapped his forehead. "Of course! We've been heading for San Miguel and she said San Pedro. We'd better turn around and get going."

Zoe didn't need to be told twice. Soon the dinghy was scooting over the waves. They were relieved to see the cruiser continue on its course for the bay.

"We didn't need that delay," said Zoe. "But nice job, getting us out of a difficult situation. Now that they're gone, we can search for Fingal again."

"First I'm going to check where the hurricane is," said Ben. He called up the satelite weather map on his BUG.

Zoe peered over his shoulder. "They were right," she said. "The storm is just northeast of here now. I didn't think it would come so close! But we'll avoid it if we don't go too far from shore. Any sign of Fingal?"

"The limpet's picking up a faint dolphin sound," said Ben. "I'll see if it matches his call."

Ben tapped at the keys. He pumped his fist in the air as the result came up. "It's a match!" Ben stared at the expanse of blue water. "He's out there somewhere."

"But how are we ever going to catch up with him?" Zoe said.

"I don't know," said Ben. "Unless . . ." He tapped at the BUG keyboard again.

"Unless what?" asked Zoe.

"Do you remember the Mundo Marino website?" Ben asked. Zoe nodded. "I looked at it again while we were on the plane," Ben said. "There was a lot of info from when the park was well run about how the dolphins were trained. There was something we might be able to use to get Fingal to come to us."

"Really?" Zoe asked eagerly.

"The website said that if the dolphins ever escaped out to sea, then their trainers could set off a sort of pinger," Ben said. "The dolphins were trained to come to the sound immediately. Perhaps we could do the same."

Zoe's face went from excited to miserable. "You've forgotten something," she said. "We don't have a pinger."

"The BUG can imitate one!" Ben said excitedly. "I can set it to send out the call."

"How?" demanded Zoe. "We don't even know what it sounded like."

"That's where you're wrong, Captain," Ben said. "There was a sound clip on the website. I remember thinking it sounded just like the timer on the stove at home."

"We've certainly heard that a lot!" Zoe said. "But what if the frequency is wrong, or the interval between the pings is off? Then Fingal won't recognize it."

"I'll keep adjusting the sound until he does," said Ben. "I know it's a long shot, Zoe, but it's our only chance at finding him."

"You're right," said Zoe. "It's worth a try! I'll keep the dinghy steady." She pulled out the first-aid kit. "After I've fixed to your hand, that is. We don't want to attract any more predators." She stuck a waterproof bandage over the cut.

Concentrating, Ben fiddled with the controls until he got the BUG's limpet to make a pinging sound. He and Zoe scanned the waves for the young dolphin.

After a few moments, nothing happened. "I'll try a different pitch," Ben said.

He tried a new setting. Then another. And another. But there was no sign of Fingal.

Zoe adjusted the sails. A stiff breeze was shaking the boat, so she had to work hard to keep it steady.

"It was a good idea," Zoe said. "But it's not working."

Ben's face was tight. "We can't give up," he muttered through clenched teeth. He adjusted the sound again. "Let's try that. Now it's time for lunch. Pass me one of those pastelitos, please."

They ate their pastries and fruit and washed them down with water. There was a fresh wind in their faces now, and small clouds were sailing across the sky.

Zoe packed up the leftover food and scanned the waves, hoping to see some sign of Fingal. "He's not going to come," she said at last. "I'll direct us back toward the shore. Maybe he's returned to the bay." She turned the dinghy toward San Miguel.

"Look!" Ben shouted suddenly. "What's that?"

A gray shape was speeding toward them through the water, leaping and plunging through the waves. It dived under the dinghy, flipping up its tail, and sending a spray of water all over Ben and Zoe.

The dolphin let out high-pitched squeaks, its scar clearly visible. "Nice job, Ben!" cried Zoe. "Your pinger worked. It's Fingal!"

CHAPTER 9

FINGAL

Fingal swam around Ben and Zoe's dinghy, leaping happily in and out of the waves.

"He's really happy to see us!" Zoe said with delight.

"He's showing us his tricks," said Ben. "Look!"

With his next leap, the young dolphin gave a flip in the air before plunging back into the waves.

When he surfaced, he gazed eagerly at the children. Zoe clapped and cheered. This seemed to please Fingal. His following jump involved two elegant spins and a flip.

"I think that calls for a reward," said Ben. "On the website it said a whistle from the trainer means the dolphin's done well. They start with a whistle and food treats at the same time. Then they wean the dolphin off the food rewards so they respond just to the whistle."

Ben put his fingers to his mouth and blew a shrill whistle. Fingal swam up to the boat and began to nod his head vigorously, making a loud chattering noise.

"He's young," Zoe said with a laugh. "He probably still associates the whistle with food. Take the tiller while I give him a treat."

Zoe pulled a dolphin snack out of her backpack held it in the air. "Here, Fingal," she called. Fingal leaped up from the water and took it cleanly from her fingers.

Fingal danced backward across the waves on his tail. "He seems to like it," said Zoe. "He's showing us what he can do so we'll give him some more. Smart boy!"

"We'll run out at this rate," said Ben. "I'll try the whistle without the treat." He whistled again.

This time Fingal swam close and laid his head on the side of the dinghy next to Zoe's hand. She reached over and stroked his smooth, cold nose and the dome of his head.

"You are a lovely boy," she crooned. "Soon you'll be safe and sound at the sanctuary."

"Keep him there if you can, Zoe," said Ben, taking out his BUG and scrolling through the menu. "This is a great time to tag him with a tracking dart. Then we won't lose him again."

Ben aimed the BUG at Fingal. But at that moment a gust of wind caught him off guard and the dart embedded itself into the wooden side of the dinghy.

"Nice shot!" Zoe said with a laugh. "Now we'll be able to track our boat! That'll be useful."

Ben stuck out his tongue at her and aimed again. This time the tiny dart flew straight into Fingal's back. The young dolphin didn't seem to notice at all. He rolled playfully in the sea. Zoe bent over the side to stroke him again, and he blasted her with water from his blowhole.

Fingal tossed his head back and chirped as if he was chuckling.

"That must be one of his tricks!" Ben said as Zoe wiped her face.

"He likes all the attention," she said happily. "We're earning his trust. Our next job is to take him somewhere that's safe and quiet and contact Uncle Stephen."

"There's an inlet a few miles away," said Ben, studying the satellite map on his BUG screen. "It's northeast of here. It seems remote, no houses or anything, but there's a small road leading down to it so the people from the Agua Clara Dolphin Sanctuary will be able to get a truck to our location."

"Sounds perfect," said Zoe, grabbing the tiller and sail ropes. "I'll sail and you keep throwing him treats so he'll follow us."

Fingal swam around the boat, leaping among the waves.

Zoe smiled. "He's like a puppy that knows it's going for a walk," she said.

Ben zoomed in on his map to get a close-up of the area. "Don't go too near the land," he warned. "The BUG's showing that the water soon gets shallow with hidden rocks. We don't want to crash into one."

"No problem," said Zoe, turning the dinghy out to sea and heading northeast.

Fingal swam alongside the boat as it gained speed. Now and again, he would soar high into the air, twist, and turn before diving back into the waves. Ben rewarded him each time with a whistle.

A sudden strong gust of wind hit Zoe in the face, taking her breath away.

The boat lurched on the choppy swell.

"What's up with Fingal?" said Ben. "He's hanging back. Maybe he's scared to stray into unfamiliar waters."

The young dolphin had stopped a few yards behind the dinghy and was calling anxiously to them. Ben threw a dolphin treat into the water.

Fingal watched as it fell, but didn't move forward to eat it. He edged backwards in the water, as if he was going to swim away at any minute.

"Come on, Fingal," said Zoe.

"I'll try his pinger," said Ben, pressing the buttons on his BUG.

He watched the sleek, rounded back of the little dolphin swimming slowly up and down just under the surface.

"We can't let him go back to the bay," Ben said. "We don't have a good way to keep him away from the fishing boats." He trailed a treat in the water. "He's nosing at my hand," he said.

"Good boy, Fingal," called Zoe.

There was a blast of wind across the bow.

The sails flapped alarmingly and the boat lurched to one side. Zoe acted quickly to bring the dinghy around until the sails filled again and the boat steadied itself.

"Look ahead, Ben," she said anxiously.

"I hope that's not the hurricane," Ben said. "It was forecast to miss San Miguel, but we don't know how close it will come to the shore."

The twins peered at the horizon. Swelling waves were rolling in toward the shore. The waves were topped with white flecks. Ominous clouds loomed overhead in the distance.

"We're going to get caught in the storm if we stay here," said Ben grimly.

Ben turned to throw another treat into the water.

But all Ben could see was the young dolphin speeding away from them.

"Fingal must have sensed the danger," Ben said. "If he's running away from the hurricane, then so should we."

CHAPTER 10

SEVERE WEATHER

Ben checked his BUG for Fingal's tracking signal. It showed an orange pulsing light moving swiftly through the water away from their dinghy back the way they'd come.

"He's heading for the bay," Ben said, worried. "And that could be dangerous. Any fishing boats will be making for San Miguel if the hurricane's getting closer."

Zoe pushed the tiller away and set a new course back toward the fishing village.

Ben checked his BUG again. "Fingal's signal shows he's swimming out to sea now, but at least he's heading south, away from the storm — and San Miguel."

Zoe brought the dinghy around and set a course to follow the little dolphin. She glanced over at Ben's BUG. "I hope we can catch up with him," she said. "Dolphins can swim fast when they want to."

The clouds had spread across the sky now. As they sailed further from the shore, the children could feel the wind growing stronger. The dinghy lurched violently.

"I'm trying to get us moving faster," said Zoe. "Hang on tight. Even though we're sailing away from the hurricane, this wind's still getting worse. I can barely hold the tiller steady."

Ben brought up the satellite forecast on his BUG. "Bad news," he said. "We're sailing right into the edge of the storm. It's going to get pretty choppy here for a while."

Zoe yelped in surprise as a sudden gust nearly tore the mainsail sheet from her grasp. She could feel the first lashings of rain on her face.

"We have to get to shore!" Ben shouted over the roaring wind.

"Too risky," Zoe shouted back. "We don't know if there are hidden rocks."

"You're the boss," answered Ben. "What do you want me to do?"

"Take the jib," Zoe yelled. "Pull that sheet until the sail stops flapping. I'll deal with the rest."

Pulling on the jib sheet with one hand, Ben adjusted his BUG to set the pinger going at full volume. The sky was even darker now, and the rain was hammering down.

"I'm keeping Fingal's signal going," Ben shouted over the sound of the wind and rain. "Dolphins have fantastic hearing."

The force of a high wave suddenly snatched the tiller from Zoe's hands. "Look out!" she cried. "Duck!"

Ben threw himself down just in time. The boom lifted and whipped across the boat with a sharp crack.

The dinghy keeled over, the mast nearly touching the waves. Then, caught by the wind, it lurched over the other way, sending the children sprawling across the deck.

"We're out of control!" cried Zoe. "We've got to get the sails down, and fast. Take the tiller and steer into the wind if you can."

Ben grabbed hold as Zoe scrambled over to the mast.

She released the mainsail, lowering it as fast as she could. Then she did the same with the jib.

Ben was struggling with the tiller. "I don't know how much longer I can hold on to this," he yelled. The dinghy bucked and tossed in the waves.

"Don't worry," Zoe shouted. "It'll be better when we've got a sea anchor."

"But there isn't an anchor in the boat!" cried Ben.

"I know," she said. "I'm going to make one."

Zoe pulled out the bailing bucket and untied the rope from its hook. She leaned out over the bow and tied the rope to the mooring handle right on the front of the boat.

"Are you crazy?" shouted Ben. "That's no good as an anchor. It won't even reach the bottom."

"It doesn't have to," said Zoe. She heaved the bucket into the sea. Immediately they felt the tug of the boat on the taut rope as it was blown around to face the oncoming waves.

They breathed a sigh of relief as the dinghy rode the next swell. "A sea anchor creates a drag," Zoe explained. "It makes us point into the wind and waves so we won't get blown around as much. When we learned about this in my sailing class, I never thought I'd be using it for real."

"I get it," said Ben. "It acts like a brake when the wind and water try to push the dinghy backward."

"Exactly," replied Zoe, shielding her eyes from the rain. "Now we both have to get down as low as possible and stay in the center."

Ben lay down and started digging through his pack.

"What are you doing?" yelled Zoe.

"We should put our flippers on," Ben yelled back. "Just in case."

They'd just gotten the flippers strapped to their feet when Ben glanced up. What he saw froze him to the spot.

A huge wave was speeding toward them. It towered over them, its top spraying with angry, white foam.

Zoe could feel the swirl of a strong undercurrent trying to pull the dinghy around.

The dinghy crested the next wave, and lurched so violently that it seemed it would snap in half. Now they were plummeting into a deep trough and the huge wave was upon them. She pulled desperately on the tiller.

But it was too late. The boat was caught up by the fierce swell. A moment later, it flipped sideways and turned right over. Zoe felt the whip of ropes and sails and managed to take a desperate breath before she was flung into the dark, churning water.

Despite her life jacket, Zoe was being tumbled around in the towering waves. No sooner did she feel air on her face than she was rolled back under. Then a wave pushed her up and she felt herself bursting into the air.

Zoe breathed deeply and let herself float on the swell. She looked around desperately for her brother, but all she could see were dark, ominous waves that lifted her up high and sucked her down again.

There was no sign of Ben anywhere.

CHAPTER 11

LOST AT SEA

"Ben!" shouted Zoe, hearing the panic in her own voice. "Ben! Where are you?!"

A jumble of thoughts went through her head. Had her brother been swept farther out to sea by the current? Had he jumped clear of the boat? Was he caught inside it, unable to free himself?

Zoe had a moment of cold, paralyzing horror. Wherever he was in this terrible sea, she had little chance of rescuing him. But she shook those fears away. She knew she had to try to find him.

She scanned the waves. It was a terrifying sight. Each swell looked bigger than the one before, and as she looked for her brother, the wind was blowing the rain hard into her face until her cheeks hurt. The black clouds were still overhead, making it so dark that it was impossible to see very far.

Then a faint cry reached her. Zoe turned herself around in the water and saw a dark shape being thrown around in the waves.

Zoe struggled to make her way to him, feeling herself being sucked back the whole time by the currents. She could see Ben's arms thrashing through the water. At last, he was near enough for her to grab on to his life jacket.

"You're okay!" Zoe could hardly get the words out in her relief.

"Just barely," shouted her brother over the roar of the storm. "Now what?"

"Find the boat!" yelled Zoe. "We need something to hold."

"Didn't it sink?" Ben asked.

"Flotation tank," Zoe said. "It keeps the boat on the surface. And with any luck, the backpacks will still be attached."

"So we just have to locate it, then," Ben said.

"Easy!" shouted Zoe. "You tagged it, remember."

"Ha!" Ben said. He tried to punch the air, but just choked on a mouthful of water.

Zoe pulled her BUG out of the water, feeling a surge of relief that it was still safely secured to her diving belt.

Zoe wiped her wet hair from her eyes and brought up the tracking screen. "It's pretty far away!" she called, watching the orange light in the water that marked the dinghy's position. "But we have to try to reach it. This way."

Fighting the storm currents, they tried to make headway through the dark water.

Finally, Zoe slowed and treaded water. "My lungs are burning," she said, panting loudly. "I need a rest."

"Agreed," said Ben. They lay their heads back on their life jackets, holding hands to stay together while riding the waves.

"The waves seem to be getting calmer now," said Ben.

"You're right," said Zoe. "Look, over there — there's a break in the clouds."

Ben looked up. Thin beams of sunlight could be seen filtering through the clouds.

"You still have your BUG, right?" asked Zoe.

"Safely tied to my belt," said Ben. "But the limpet's with the boat, so there's no point in sending out a call to Fingal. He'd go there instead of coming to us."

"He's probably far away by now," said Zoe, "but we can still check his tracking signal."

Just then, something heavy slammed into their legs. Ben and Zoe looked down in alarm.

A smiling dolphin face popped up from the waves in front of them. A scar ran down from its right eye. It was Fingal. The young dolphin chirped loudly. Then he walked backward on his tail and came swimming back to them.

Zoe stroked his side as he swam past. "We're so glad to see you," she cried. "Now that the hurricane's moved on, you've come to find us!"

Suddenly, the water all around them began to seethe.

In an instant, the twins were surrounded by sleek gray bodies, arcing and diving through the waves.

"It's a pod of dolphins," said Ben. "Fingal seems to have made friends with them."

Fingal was leaping among the group. "They're getting too close for comfort," Zoe shouted above the chirps. "They're circling us. I'm sure they're just playing, but we'll have trouble getting past them."

The dolphins were swimming right up to Ben and Zoe now, forming a tight band around them. They felt their arms and legs being wrapped by the strong flippers. Ben held out his arms to fend them off.

"I don't think they're playing," he said anxiously. "We should try to break through before we get hurt."

As a tail passed him, he kicked hard, hoping to burst through the gap, but at once another dolphin was on him, pushing him back to Zoe with its nose.

"I've got a bad feeling about this," he yelled. "Remember that show about dolphins that attacked and ate seals?"

Zoe looked at him in horror. "We're in big trouble!" she said.

CHAPTER 12

SWIM FOR YOUR LIFE

They tried to fend off the dolphins, pushing against the strong bodies. "Fingal's still with them," yelled Ben. "Look, here he comes. He won't hurt us."

But the young dolphin began to join in with the jostling. The circle got even tighter.

"We're going to be crushed!" shouted Zoe.

Suddenly, between the troughs in the waves, Ben could just see another fin cutting through the water toward them.

"There's a shark out there!" Ben cried.

Now Zoe understood what the pod was doing. "They're protecting us," she said. "They're guarding us from the shark. And Fingal's helping them."

Two of the dolphins peeled away from the pod and swam straight for the shark.

There was a tremendous splash as the three huge creatures crashed together.

"What's happening?" yelled Ben.

"I can't see," Zoe yelled back. "They must be ramming it."

Their dolphin protectors continued to swim around them. Fingal gave them a reassuring nudge with his nose as he passed. Then the two dolphins were back. The pod was suddenly giving urgent chirps and squeaks.

"They must have chased it away," Ben shouted. "There's no sign —"

To Zoe's horror, he cried out and disappeared under the water.

The dolphins dived frantically. Zoe tried to follow, but the life jacket kept her on the surface. She tore at the straps, flung it off, and dived, searching for her brother.

Once she saw him, the blood turned to ice in her veins. The shark had swum under the pod and was biting one of Ben's flippers, shaking him like a rag doll. Zoe swam down and tried to pull Ben away. But she was no match for the huge shark.

Zoe kicked down hard with her heel and whacked the shark on its nose. The shark recoiled, letting go of the flipper. Zoe grabbed Ben's life jacket and made for the surface as the shark lunged again.

The shark's mouth was open wide, showing rows of sharp, deadly teeth. Suddenly, something sleek and gray shot across and rammed the shark hard in the side of its face.

It was Fingal. The shark reeled at the blow.

Ben's life jacket was pulling him up to the surface. Zoe swam up beside him.

"I didn't see it coming!" cried Ben.

They peered anxiously into the depths. Dark shapes were flashing back and forth in a desperate frenzy as the other dolphins joined Fingal in attacking the shark.

"We need to get away from here," said Zoe. "But how?"

A gray streamlined body pushed in between them and leaped into the air.

The figure swam around and came up to them, a happy grin on its scarred face. Their young friend nudged them with his nose. Then he swam around and came up behind them, lifting their arms as he passed. He did it again.

"What's he doing?" said Ben.

"He wants us to grab his dorsal fin," said Zoe. "I think he's going to give us a tow!"

As Fingal went to pass them again, they grasped his back fin, and at once felt his strength and speed as he pulled them through the water.

"I don't really care where we go," Ben shouted back, spluttering a little as the foamy waves splashed in his face. "As long as it's far away from that shark."

Fingal swam strongly, keeping his fin just above the surface of the water. Zoe's hand began to feel numb from hanging on for so long, but Fingal seemed tireless. Then a worry began to form in her head.

"He's only ever lived in a pool," Zoe said to Ben. "He could be swimming in circles."

"You're right," Ben called back. "But what else can we do? There's a hungry shark out there somewhere and —" Ben stopped talking and wiped the water from his eyes. "Do you see what I see?"

"What?" Zoe asked, trying to peer ahead. "What is it?"

"Palm trees!" Ben cried.

CHAPTER 13

LAND

"Is it the shore?" asked Zoe. She could see the tops of the green trees now, the sun shining brightly on them through the widening gap in the clouds.

"It's the coral island," said Ben. "Fingal brought us to safety."

The dolphin slowed a little way from where the island rose out of the sea. Ben and Zoe released his fin, and he disappeared underneath the water. He resurfaced in an arcing dive nearby.

As Ben and Zoe swam toward the land, Ben peered down at the wonderful colors of the coral beneath them.

"I win!" said Zoe, as she reached the shore. She pulled off her flippers and stumbled out of the sea. "Paradise!" Zoe declared, throwing herself down on the sand underneath a palm tree.

"We'd better let Erika know where we are!" said Ben. He got out of the water and flopped down beside her. "Then she can contact Uncle Stephen so the center will come and get Fingal while he's still here. We'll have to hide when they come, of course." He clicked the quick-dial key on his BUG.

"Hello!" came Erika's voice. "What news do you have for me?" Ben told her everything that had happened.

"Fingal's here with us and he's tagged," Ben finished. "So if Uncle Stephen can call the Agua Clara Dolphin Sanctuary . . ."

"I'm on it," came Erika's calm voice. "Your BUG's giving me your location. I'll come and get you. We can retrieve your sailing dinghy later."

Ben stretched out on the sand. "No need to hurry!" he said.

Erika laughed. "I'm afraid you can't be there when the sanctuary people turn up," she said. "See you soon." She hung up.

Ben jumped up and gazed out to sea. "The pod's back," he said. "Looks like they've scared away the shark."

The dolphins leaped and dived in the waves, glittering in the sunshine.

"I wish we could thank them," said Zoe.

Ben nodded. "They saved our lives," he said. "With Fingal's help, of course."

Fingal gave a series of calls and began to swim toward the pod. But then he whipped around and headed back toward the island. He chirped and walked backward on his tail, as if he was in one of his shows back at the marine park.

"I've been thinking," said Ben. "It does seem like a shame to have him taken to a sanctuary, no matter how nice it is. He's getting used to the ocean and he seems to have found a pod without any help."

Zoe nodded. "Maybe the best thing for him would be to stay here, but how could we be sure he'd stay with them?" She sounded worried. "He could go back to bothering the fishing boats and get into danger."

Ben and Zoe watched Fingal cutting through the waves, clicking and chirping.

Ben sighed. "What if Fingal is too used to people?" he wondered aloud. "The sanctuary might help him change that behavior."

Suddenly, the pod came closer to Fingal, calling and chirping. The young dolphin called back, nodding his snout. "Go on, boy," said Zoe. "Go with them."

But Fingal swam closer to the island. The pod kept up their calls. Then one of the larger dolphins broke away from the group and swam slowly toward Fingal. The children saw the two gray bodies dance around each other under the water.

"That's it, boy," urged Ben. "They won't hurt you."

The older dolphin made its way back to the pod, swimming in sync with the other dolphins. But Fingal still didn't follow.

At last, the dolphins turned and headed off toward the deep ocean. Then Fingal slipped underwater.

"Where did he go?" asked Zoe. "I can't see him."

"There he is!" exclaimed Ben. He pointed at a sleek shape moving like a torpedo toward the pod. Almost immediately, the figure caught up to the other dolphins and joined them.

Zoe shielded her eyes. "Fingal reached the other dolphins!" she cried. "Look, he's playing with them."

They watched as Fingal and his new family swam off into the distance.

The pod of dolphins swam together, playing, splashing, and jumping over each other. They looked like one big family.

"Better call Erika again," said Ben, with a grin. "We're the only ones who need rescuing now."

CHAPTER 14

HOME SWEET HOME

Later that week, Zoe and Ben were
resting in their grandma's back yard and
reading magazines. Grandma was in
the kitchen, making one of her famous
chocolate cakes to celebrate their successful
mission.

Zoe turned to face Ben. "There's an
article here about sailing," she said with
a grin. "Wanna take some lessons this
summer?"

"I don't need sailing lessons anymore," said Ben proudly. "I could teach a class on how to lift a capsized dinghy upright again. And how to bail it out! After all, I've had first-hand experience now."

"You did really well," said Zoe, nodding proudly. "The boat-rental woman had no idea what her dinghy had been through when we finally took it back to her in one piece."

Not long after Fingal had left with his new pod, Erika had sped up to the coral island in a rented motorboat. They'd tracked down the capsized dinghy and Zoe had shown Ben how to stand on the keel to pull the vessel upright. The trusty bucket had proved very useful in bailing all the water out. It took a lot of work, but eventually they were sailing the waves, heading back toward shore.

"Erika was really pleased with the response to Uncle Stephen's nets," said Zoe. "Especially in San Miguel. They were really excited to give them a try."

"Especially that fisherman who started telling everyone about his encounter with the super-dolphin in the bay," Ben joked.

"The one that had teeth like knives and cut its way through his net?" Zoe laughed.

Ben nodded and chuckled. "Yeah," he said. "He'll be repeating that big fish tale for the rest of his life."

Zoe snorted laughter. "It was so funny I nearly forgot to pretend I didn't understand a word," she said.

They heard the phone ring in the house. After a few moments, Grandma poked her head out of the window. "That was your uncle," she called. "He said it's urgent."

Zoe jumped up in surprise. "Another mission so soon?" she said.

Grandma shook her head. "No," she said. "He told me to turn the TV on right away!"

They ran inside and crowded around the television in the kitchen.

A news program cut from a weather forecast to show a newscaster sitting at a desk. "Thanks, Doris," he said, turning to face the camera.

The newscaster shuffled some papers and smiled wide. "And last but definitely not least," he said, "we've heard about a strange turn of events in the Caribbean. A group of wild dolphins have been entertaining tourists with some rather amazing tricks."

The camera cut from the studio and to an expanse of blue water. A pod of dolphins were leaping to and fro in the waves. Suddenly, two adult dolphins began to walk backward on their tails just like Fingal had done.

A reporter appeared on screen wearing a pair of swim trunks and a tank top.

"I have Monica Vasquez from the Agua Clara Dolphin Sanctuary with me," he said. "Can you tell me what this is all about?"

A pretty, dark-haired woman came into view. "There was a bottlenose dolphin from a marine park dumped in the sea recently," she told the camera. "We were alerted to his plight and were going to take him to the center for rehabilitation, but we soon got a message saying that he'd been adopted by a local pod. They're teaching him how to live in the wild, and it seems he is teaching them a few tricks, too."

The camera zoomed in as another dolphin reared up on its tail and walked backward, slicing through the waves. Onlookers cheered and clapped.

"See that scar under its eye?" cried Zoe, pointing to the screen. "It's Fingal!"

"He should have a better life now," said Ben with a big smile on his face. "Lots of fish whenever he wants them, and no whistles to perform to. And although we needed that ride, I hope he never has to tow a human again."

"One thing's for sure," said Zoe. "He's finally found a home."

THE AUTHORS

Jan Burchett and **Sara Vogler** were already friends when they discovered they both wanted to write children's books, and that it was much more fun to do it together. They have since written over a hundred and thirty stories ranging from educational books and stories for younger readers to young adult fiction. They have written for series such as Dinosaur Cove and Beast Quest, and they are authors of the Gargoylz books.

THE ILLUSTRATOR

Diane Le Feyer discovered a passion for drawing and animation at the age of five. In 2002, she graduated with honors from the Ecole Emile Cohl school of design. Diane worked as a character designer, 3D modeler, and animator in the video games industry before joining the Cartoon Saloon animation studio, where she worked as a director, animator, illustrator, and character designer. Diane was also a part of the early design and development of the movie *The Secret of Kells*.

GLOSSARY

capsize (KAP-size)—to turn over in the water

dinghy (DING-ee)—a small, open boat

hologram (HOL-uh-gram)—an image made by laser beams that looks three-dimensional

mast (MAST)—a tall pole that stands on the deck of a boat or ship and supports its sails

mechanism (MEK-uh-niz-uhm)—a system of moving parts inside a machine

monitoring (MON-uh-tur-ing)—regularly checking something over a period of time

operative (OP-er-uh-tiv)—a secret agent or spy

pod (POD)—a small herd or school of seals, whales, or dolphins

rehabilitation (ree-hab-bil-uh-TAY-shuhn)—the act of restoring a person or animal's health and safety

sanctuary (SANGK-choo-er-ee)—a safe and protected place for endangered animals

BOTTLENOSE DOLPHIN
STATUS: REGIONALLY THREATENED

Bottlenose dolphins are found all over the world in temperate or tropical waters. They have no gills and cannot breathe underwater, so they must regularly surface to get air. While the dolphin isn't endangered, their livelihood is still very much at risk from:

FISHING: Some fishing nets are big enough to accidentally catch dolphins. Getting trapped in the nets can kill or maim the dolphins.

PREDATORS: Some larger sharks, like tiger sharks or great white sharks, will hunt and kill dolphins. Orca whales have been known to attack dolphins as well. In Japan and the Faroe Islands, dolphins are killed for their meat.

POLLUTION: Factory waste and farm fertilizers sometimes get washed into the sea, where they can harm or kill dolphins.

BUT IT'S NOT ALL BAD FOR THE BOTTLENOSE DOLPHIN! Nature-saving organizations the world over are working with fishermen to help reduce the number of dolphins, sharks, and turtles that they accidentally catch in their fishing nets. A few countries have banned the hunting of bottlenose dolphins, and the animals have a special protected status in European law.

DISCUSSION QUESTIONS

1. Ben and Zoe love animals. Do you have any animals as pets? What kinds? Talk about your pets.

2. The twins almost get caught in a hurricane. What's the worst weather you've ever experienced? What happened?

3. Of all the fun things Ben and Zoe do in this book, which one would you most like to be a part of? Why?

WRITING PROMPTS

1. Ben and Zoe travel all over the world. If you could travel anywhere, where would you go? What would you see? How would you get there? Write about your trip.

2. Fingal knew how to do some impressive tricks because of the training he received. Design your own dolphin trick. How does it work? How would you train the dolphin to perform it? Write about it.

3. If you could save any kind of animal from danger, what animal would you choose? Write a short story about rescuing a wild animal.